MANGO, ABUELA, and ME

Meg Medina

illustrated by **Angela Dominguez**

CANDLEWICK PRESS

SHE COMES TO US in winter, leaving behind her sunny
house that rested between two snaking rivers.

"Her old place was too much for just one," Mami tells me
as we make room in my dresser for her clothes.

"And too far away for us to help," Papi adds. "Abuela
belongs with us now, Mia."

But I still feel shy when I meet this far-away grandmother.

¡Pín pán pún!

Papi unfolds Abuela's bed, and slides it right next to mine. "You will get to know each other," he says.

But when I show Abuela my new book, she can't unlock the English words. We can only look at the pictures and watch Edmund race on his wheel.

Then, just before we turn out the light, she pulls out two things tucked inside the satin pocket of her suitcase.

A feather—*una pluma*—from a wild parrot that roosted in her mango trees and a snapshot—*una fotografía*—of a young man with Papi's smile.

Tu abuelo, she says, climbing into bed.

Snuggled in my pajamas, I smell flowers in her hair, sugar and cinnamon baked into her skin.

That night, I dream of a red bird circling in the sky.

The rest of the winter, while Mami and Papi are at work, Abuela waits for me to get home from school. Then we bundle up in thick socks and handmade sweaters to walk to the park and toss bread to the sparrows.

My *español* is not good enough to tell her the things an *abuela* should know. Like how I am the very best in art and how I can run as fast as the boys.

And her English is too *poquito* to tell me all the stories
I want to know about Abuelo and the rivers that ran right
outside their door.

With our mouths as empty as our bread baskets, we walk
back home and watch TV.

"Abuela and I can't understand each other," I whisper to Mami.

"Things will get better," Mami says. "Remember how it was with Kim?"

Kim is my best friend at school. When she was new, our whole class helped teach her English words. Now Miss Wilson sometimes has to say, "Please be quiet, girls. Others are working."

After school the next day, while Abuela and I are making meat pies for our snack, I pretend I am Miss Wilson.

"Dough," I say, pointing to the ball.

Abuela says, "Dough. *Masa,*" and rolls it flat.

"Masa," I say.

She drops a spoonful of meat in place. *"Carne."*

"Carne," I say. "Meat."

"Pasas." "Raisins!"

"Aceite." "Oil!"

Then I remember the word cards we taped in our classroom to help Kim. So, while Abuela fries our *empanadas*, I put up word cards, too, until everything is covered — even Edmund.

Soon we are playing *Oye y Di* — Hear and Say — all around the house.

But that night, she still calls my pillow a "palo" and she says Edmund is a "gángster."

"We'll keep practicing," I whisper.

But the next day, I cannot practice with Abuela after all. Edmund has run out of his favorite seeds, so Mami and I have to ride the bus downtown to buy more.

Sometimes there are kittens sleeping in the pet-shop window. But when we arrive this time, something even better is behind the glass.

"Look!" I say. The window has become a jungle filled with birds! And right in the middle is a parrot staring at us with black-bean eyes.

I press my nose to the glass, thinking of the red feather Abuela gave me.

"Let's buy him!" I tell Mami.

"But Mia, you already have Edmund!" Mami says.

"Oh, not for me," I say. "For Abuela. Like the parrot that lived in her mango trees! He can keep her company when I'm at school."

When we bring him home to Abuela, she says, *"¡Un loro!"*—a parrot! We name him Mango, because his wings are green, orange, and gold, like the fruit.

During the day, Abuela teaches him how to give beaky kisses and to bob his head when she sings "Los Pollitos" to him.

"Buenas tardes, Mango," Abuela says, opening his cage door when I get home from school.

"Good afternoon," I say, and give him a seed. Soon Mango calls to me even before we open his cage.

"¡Buenas tardes!" he says when I open the door. "Good afternoon!"

Abuela, Mango, and I practice new words every day. *Mi español* gets faster and Abuela and Mango learn the days of the week, all the months of the year, and the names of coins.

"How did he learn all that?" Papi asks when we show him all that Mango can do. Abuela winks at me and gives Mango a piece of banana, peel and all.

"Practice," she says.

Before long, Abuela asks me how to say harder things, too, so she can talk with the neighbors who stop by.

Has the mailman come?

It is chilly today.

Can I get you some cookies and lemonade?

Soon, when friends stop by to see Mango's latest tricks, they can understand everything Abuela says.

But best of all, now when Abuela and I are lying next to each other in our beds, our mouths are full of things to say. I tell her about my *buen día* and show her my best *pintura* of Mango.

Abuela reads my favorite book with only a little help, and she tells me new stories about Abuelo, who could dive for river stones with a single breath and weave a roof out of palms. I draw pictures for her. She still misses their old house, she says, but now only a little bit.

Mango listens to us from his perch until my eyes grow heavy.

"*Hasta mañana*, Abuela," I say.

Abuela kisses me. "Good night, Mia."

"*Hasta mañana*. Good night," Mango calls.

And soon we all fall asleep.

For Christina, Sandra, and Alex —
and the *abuelas* who loved them
M. M.

To my family, and to my buddy Erika for all her help
A. D.

First edition 2015

Library of Congress Catalog Card Number 2014951415
ISBN 978-0-7636-6900-3

15 16 17 18 19 20 CCP 10 9 8 7 6 5 4 3 2 1

Printed in Shenzhen, Guangdong, China

This book was typeset in ITC Esprit.
The illustrations were done in ink, gouache, and marker,
with a sprinkling of digital magic.

Candlewick Press
99 Dover Street
Somerville, Massachusetts 02144

visit us at www.candlewick.com